After the Twa Corbies

and Other Stories

The Stansted Mountfitchet

Creative Writing Group

Printed and bound in Great Britain by
Catford Print Centre

Cover designed by Andrew Jennings from an original painting by John Conder

Illustrations by John Conder

Edited by Yvonne Ayres, Allan James, Elizabeth Jennings & Sally Rich

First Published 2024 by The Stansted Mountfitchet Creative Writing Group

stanstedcreativewritinggroup@gmail.com

ISBN Number 978-1-0369-0303-9

Contents

Weathering the Storm

Elizabeth Jennings

Cold. Not just cold, but bitingly cold. The sort of day when the chill goes through to the bones and breath makes spectacles misty. Although Malcolm, a well-built man, was wearing several layers under his waxed jacket he could still feel it. Shivering, he walked faster, surprising his dog, Bear, who hastened his pace to a trot to keep up with the lead, which was so taut there was no opportunity to sniff. 'Doesn't he know dogs need to sniff as part of their exercise?' thought the over-sized, curly-coated Labrador.

Wind chill factor came to Malcolm's mind as he pulled his hat down over his ears and the old college scarf across his mouth. The wind was coming in from the sea, roughing it up, sometimes hitting the wall of the promenade with a resounding thud, sparkles of salty water accosting him through the air. He moved to the back of the path, dragging the resistant dog with him. Bear, realising there was a grass verge this side of the path, suddenly speeded up to get a quick draught of previous animals' scents before his master noticed. At least having a dog made Malcolm go for a walk in all weathers. Left to himself he'd have stayed at home this morning in the warmth of his study, trying to get a handle on his latest venture – an online writing course. Apparently, so his wife said, lockdown was an ideal opportunity to 'improve his mind'. Did his mind need improving? Moot point.

Malcolm and Linda had met at school, went to different universities, married at 21, two kids, four grandchildren, now both retired from teaching and enjoying life. Linda was an enthusiastic volunteer: lively, purple-streaked hair, outrageous clothes, an ageing hippy. She was delivering food parcels to struggling families this morning.

The memorial bench facing the raging sea was occupied. Awful day for sitting Malcolm thought as he looked at the two figures: they had substantial waterproofs over them plus broad-brimmed hats to keep the rain from their eyes. Must be storm watchers. Bear tried to pull him to the bench, a discarded flask underneath, but Malcolm sped up, the whistling downpour deluging him. His eyelashes were dripping. Once home, he towelled Bear, gave him a biscuit then set to making soup. Lunch was Malcolm's job if Linda was out.

'Hi, I'm home!' called Linda, 'Foul weather, did you take Bear out in it? Lovely aroma. Soup? Let's have lunch on trays by the fire.' She hung up her wet coat and sat by the wood burner rubbing her hands together.

'Good idea. Bear and I are drying out. We saw a couple sitting out in this. Mad!'

Damp fur steaming, Bear pushed himself against Linda's legs. The wet dog smell overwhelmed her, but she patted his head. 'Poor Bear,' she said. 'You should have a doggy raincoat.'

It was an afternoon for loafing in the inherited worn leather armchairs and reading the Sunday papers, which had been spread across the room for days, unwanted pages thrown on the floor, waiting to be binned, the harbour view jigsaw puzzle on the old oak table abandoned temporarily. They didn't do tidy. As Linda said, their house was a home, not a showcase. She curled her long legs underneath her, a Christmas slipper sliding onto Bear's prone body. He twitched, barely raising his head, luxuriating in the warmth of the glowing stove.

The newspaper falling from her lap woke Linda up.

'We've missed the news: should just catch the local,' she said, turning on the TV.

The newsreader was saying there had been a tragedy on the coast. Linda turned up the volume. Likely some idiot took a boat out. People are so foolhardy when it's stormy.

'Malcolm, listen, a couple has been found dead.

Here. On the memorial bench. How awful!'

The newsreader carried on: 'Foul play is not suspected. No-one else is being sought in connection with the deaths.' And then he moved on to other news.

'But I saw them, I told you. I walked right past. They were alive then – or I assumed they were. Bear tried to pull me over to them. Oh God, could I have saved them? What happened – were they attacked? There was nobody else about that I saw.'

They sat, shocked. Malcolm went over to an antique trolley and poured two large brandies. They warmed the bowls of the glasses in their hands, huddled in silence.

It was the headline in the local paper.

SAD END TO A DEVOTED COUPLE'S LIFE

A couple in their 80s were found dead in Hastings. Police attended the seafront at 5pm on Saturday after a call from the public. The deaths are being treated as unexplained but not suspicious and the coroner has been informed.

Peter and Audrey Dubarry were found by Mark Edmunds, 17, and his friend John Perry, 18. Mark said: 'I went to see if they were all right as it was getting dark and raining hard but they didn't move. I touched him on the arm and he fell forwards. John called 999.'

A neighbour said the Dubarrys were a devoted couple. Peter was suffering from cancer and his wife had dementia. They were depressed by the lockdown.

The next week's paper carried a small item saying a note had been left telling of their suicide pact. The family said that they would have gone to their favourite spot: it was where Peter had asked Audrey to marry him almost 50 years previously. They'd had a very happy marriage and probably couldn't face the future unless they were together.

'That's so sad Malcolm,' Linda said, passing him the paper.

'Would we do that, do you think?' he asked.

'Good gracious no! If you died first, I'd get another dog, or maybe a cat.' After a few moments thought she added:

'And a gardener.'

Malcolm smiled – that was why he loved her so much. Her total sense of the ridiculous.

The Chosen

Lavinia Epworth

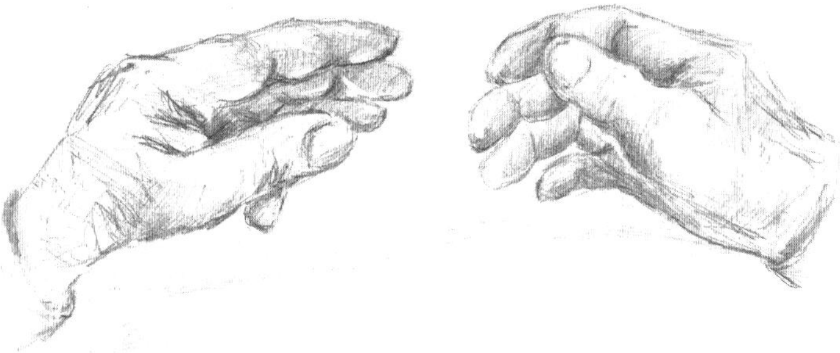

It seems like only yesterday that we met; or rather that he chose me. The room was dark and there were several of us all wanting to be picked, but he took his time. He was a man who always took his time throughout the years we were together. He was young then, but even in the years that took him into maturity his movements were always confident and measured. I felt the jealousy from the others as he ran his hands over me in his gentle way. They wanted to be with him; I knew that.

We spent a lifetime together. I loved being with him and I knew he felt the same. His wife would sometimes nag him. She didn't appreciate the skills he possessed and would often chastise him for the hours he spent with me. How do I know this? Well, he would talk to me and share the difficulties of his life in the private times we were together. I often wished she would be kinder to him. I know he worked hard providing for his family.

Sometimes he would gently spread oil on my body, often before he had to leave me in order to be with his family. I did not resent these times of absence because I knew they were important to him as well. I longed for his return and to feel his warm and gentle touch as he caressed my body as only he knew how. We had times on our own together when he worked away from home. These were a great adventure as we visited new places sharing and exploring. Through the years it was as though we moulded together, his hands knowing just how much or how little pressure he needed to use on me.

With the passage of time there were changes in him. This was inevitable. His hands became calloused and hard. Sometimes there was a tremor in his usual steady hand. He expressed frustration when he could not do the things that he could when he was younger. He was frustrated that he sometimes took longer and he still could not achieve his goal.

It was then that he introduced me to his son with his soft hands filled with uncertainty. He instructed the lad well with patience and understanding. So it was that I had a new owner and I knew that there were many more adventures to be had. I was sure that I would be cared for by this young man because we both knew that he had learned from the master. There is a saying I believe that a 'bad workman always blames his tools'. That was never going to be my fate. I was always going to be the sharpest chisel in the box because the men in my life knew how to care for me so we created beauty together.

The Camera

Allan James

'I've got this great camera,' Amy said, 'come into the garden and I'll show you.' A couple of minutes later they stood on what was left of the patio, looking at the tangled mass of weeds, overgrown shrubs and an ivy-stunted tree. 'The landscapers are in tomorrow,' Amy said, 'so this will all disappear.' She waved her hand at the overgrown mess that spread out to left and right of them. 'I thought it'd be a good idea to take some pics every day,' she grinned at her friend, 'a kind of before, during and after project.'

‘If they’re in tomorrow, you should take some now; before it all gets dug out.’ Zoe stepped off the cracked patio tile she stood on and moved across to the end of the garden. Turning towards her friend she stepped to one side then said, ‘This would be a good place to start from, it gives a pretty good view of the whole plot.’

Half an hour later they’d quartered the garden and, having agreed on a couple of vantage points, Zoe pointed to the camera. ‘What do you suppose that button’s for?’ The button, on the side of the camera body, was labelled with the letters V and R. ‘I don’t suppose it stands for Victoria Reigns!’

Amy looked at the camera, at the button in question. ‘Oh, I expect it’s the VR function. Switches from ordinary to virtual mode.’

‘Virtual mode? Is that, as in virtual reality?’ Zoe asked and thought for a moment. ‘So does that mean it takes real pictures of things that aren’t there, or does it almost take a picture of something that is there?’ She paused again, ‘Or maybe it almost takes a picture of something that’s nearly there. Does it just imagine something and take a picture of it, or maybe it takes a picture of something the photographer imagines?'

Amy watched, confused, as her friend let herself out of the garden gate. Not for the first time she wondered why Zoe had to be such a smart-arse, and did she really think it did her any favours? It didn't impress anybody and after all, she didn't really have any friends of her own, only those she knew through Amy. She shrugged, and turned back to the ruined garden, picking her way carefully through the tall overgrown stuff with purple flowers that grew in the boggy ground at the end of the garden. She reached the small lump of concrete where a sundial or something had once stood and turned to look back. She was right, a few before and after pictures would be a good idea. Maybe she'd fiddle about with them on her computer and do a Warhol-type thing with the same picture nine times in different colours. Perhaps, she thought, I could make it into a screen saver.

Amy was about to make her way back to the French windows when another of Zoe's ideas struck her. She'd said that taking a series of pictures to make a kind of stop-motion animation might be fun. Amy looked around. If, as the landscapers had said, there was a pond somewhere, which was why the ground was all boggy, then a time-lapse of it being cleared and re-built would, she thought, be nice. She took a few pictures of the area and went back inside to decide which particular view was best, and how often she'd take a picture. Every hour was out of the question but once a day seemed too long an interval. She'd have to think about it.

Rather than fiddle around with the memory card, she decided to view the pictures in the camera itself and at first, all the pictures looked much the same, a wilderness of weed. Clumps of dandelions fixed firmly to the spaces between the few flagstones of the original patio. Nettles inhabited every part of the garden and managed to somehow survive even though supporting a forest of bindweed. Ivy ran rampant over a jumble of broken brick and distressed statues. She reached for her camera and looked again at the first of the pictures. In the middle, covered in ivy and more than half hidden amidst the thistles and couch grass, was a statue of something that looked like a cherub.

She took a sip of wine and, on closer inspection, the shape looked more like Bacchus than Cupid. She looked out of the window, but dusk was falling and from where she sat it was difficult to see the spot in the garden where she'd taken the picture. Still, she didn't remember seeing anything at all when she was outside.

The next picture was much the same. A corner of the garden with a wilderness of weed coating the remains of a small building. Amy could just make out where the doorway had been and a low window to the side, but everything above that had disappeared, eaten by the ravenous weeds. She thought it odd that she hadn't noticed even so small a piece of building before and wondered if there was enough of it left to make into some kind of feature. She'd have to speak with the gardeners in the morning.

Early the next morning Amy went to the French window and set up the tripod before fixing the camera to it. She had some trouble fixing the two together but after much fumbling and swearing she managed to set it up so that she could take a picture, with the remote control, every hour without moving the camera in between shots. She discovered that her desk was also in line with the camera so she wouldn't have to get up from her computer, just set the timer, point the remote control and bingo; another picture.

The work in the garden only took a few days and the pond was one of the last things to be finished. It was with relief that Amy took the camera off the tripod and turned it on to view the images on its small screen. She hadn't realised it would all take so long, and she'd become quite impatient from about the middle of day one. It was a shame that the statues and ruin she'd seen had turned out to be nothing more than peculiar twistings and twinings of what the gardeners had called rosebay willow herb. The corner of a ruined summerhouse, or even a small cherub would have been nice. Still, she thought, she could always buy a statue and the garden was big enough for a small summerhouse. When she could afford it.

But it was finished. She could upload from the memory card onto her computer and turn them into a stunning animation. But first things first, a quick look at the images in the camera to see what they were like.

They weren't like the pictures she'd taken.

She'd taken several sharply focussed shots each day of a garden that was gradually revealing a pond and its progress towards reconstruction.

The pictures on the screen looked grainy and old, almost sepia toned. And in the very first shot, the pond was complete, shaded by tall trees and surrounded by exotic plants in well-kept gardens with neatly cut lawns. Facing the pond was a statue of Bacchus, and behind that, a building. When Amy looked more closely, she could see it was brick built with low windows, an old summerhouse or orangery.

But it was the last few pictures that made her gasp.

There was one of a figure, blurred but somehow managing to look desperate, running away from the camera, towards the pond.

In the next frame, it became clear the person was trying to escape, to get away from another figure that had suddenly come into the frame.

Then the stabbing.

Then the body being tumbled into the pond.

The body rolled over. Already smeared by streamers of blanket weed, the face of her friend, Zoe, gazed out blankly with its dull, dead eyes.

And then the last picture. The killer had stepped back from the pond, back towards the camera. Then turned. Amy stared at her own face staring back from the sepia figure in the photograph.

The Bone Gatherer

Yvonne Ayres

Pakak pauses and briefly straightens up. Massaging the aching muscles in the small of her back, she carefully studies the summer sky through narrowed eyes. Since the missionary had told her people that the world is at war, she is ever vigilant, fearful that at any time the enemy may jump from an airplane and kill them all.

Reassured that she's in no immediate danger, Pakak releases her hold on the hunting rifle constantly by her side and bends once more to the maggot covered carcass at her feet. She feels one-year-old Hanta stirring in the pouch of her caribou parka. The young Inuit looks across at the sled already containing two full sacks of bones. One more sack to fill before she can go back to their hut and prepare the evening meal. Pakak sings softly to the baby as she picks up the dog carcass, hungry maggots crawling over her bare hands.

It's one of many dog carcasses she's come across while collecting bones. Sadly her people's hunting and sled dogs are dying from an unknown disease despite everyone's best efforts to stop it spreading. Some believe it is connected to the war somehow. She and her husband, Tulok, have lost all but three of theirs. Pakak finally throws the cleaned carcass into the sack already containing dog, walrus and seal bones. The missionary said the Canadian Government needs as many bones as possible to make something for smoke for the army. She doesn't fully understand how it will help defeat the enemy but does as asked, filling her quota of three sacks each day to be shipped south. A sudden noise causes Pakak to quickly look up to the sky again, before she spots heavily pregnant Yuka waving in the distance, slowly pulling her laden sled, having no dogs left to do the job.

By the time her friend draws near Pakak has filled her last sack and lifted it onto her sled. Hanta is now wide awake and squirming in his baby pouch making every task more difficult for his mother.

'Hello little Hanta. Are you being a good boy for your mama?' coos Yuka as she smiles at the baby. The one-year-old gurgles with delight. Pakak thinks that Yuka is going to be a really good mother. Having roped the two sleds together for Pakak's dogs to haul, they make their way back to the summer camp in companionable silence. Coming from the same small, remote island and travelling the same traditional Inuit routes all over the eastern Arctic, the two young women have been friends for a long time. Their husbands are out hunting the caribou together, just as they do every year during the short summer months.

Yuka suddenly gasps and grips her side.

'Are you alright?' Pakak asks, looking concerned. Yuka nods and biting her lip stares straight ahead towards the small collection of huts just visible in the distance.

Having insisted on unloading both sleds Pakak, a trained midwife, is now inside Yuka's hut gently examining her friend. Hanta is busy exploring his surroundings, happy to be free from the restriction of his mother's amauti. 'This little one is going to appear very soon,' she remarks.

'But it's not due yet. Will it be alright?' cries an alarmed Yuka.

'Babies come whenever they're ready. It will be fine,' Pakak assures her with a smile adding 'if you remember Hanta decided to arrive very unexpectedly in the middle of my sister's wedding ceremony.' She looks fondly at her little boy just as he falls on his bottom in an attempt to run across the brightly coloured rug. Both women chuckle as Pakak scoops up the shocked toddler in her arms saying 'he arrived in a hurry and continues to do everything in a hurry.' Shaking her head she carries a now protesting Hanta back to her own dwelling. The young mother's indulgent smile fades to be replaced by a frown as her gaze is once more drawn upwards. She will not be able to relax until the men arrive safely back from the day's hunting trip.

The stew is gently bubbling and the table laid with bread, bowls and spoons. Pakak has fed Hanta, settled him in his crib, and there is still no sign of the men. She goes outside to wait. Shivering in the cold wind that signals the ending of summer, Pakak carefully watches and listens, alert to any sight or sound of the two men's return. All is silent around her, everyone else in the small community inside their huts. Just as she turns to go back to check on Hanta, Pakak hears a faint shout. She peers into the distance straining to identify the source of the sound. She waves, relief sweeping through her as she finally recognises the figure as it gets closer. Her joy is short-lived when she sees there is only one man.

'Where is Tulok?' As Yuka's husband moves towards her Pakak gasps as she spots the parka covered body on the sled. She instantly recognises the intricate embroidery that kept her occupied through the long winter months.

'How badly is he injured?' screams Pakak, as she

darts towards the sled. The young man stops her, places his gloved hands on her shoulders and says sadly,

'There is nothing to be done.' Looking up into his haggard face Pakak knew that she was about to hear the news she'd been dreading for months.

'Was it the enemy?' she whispers through chattering teeth, her whole body trembling.

'I don't know. I just found him on the ground. His heart had stopped beating. I'm so sorry.' Pakak's grief-stricken howls rent the still night air. Her neighbours rush to her side and attempt to comfort and console her. Then Yuka's husband is tugging Pakak's arm urging her to go to his wife.

At the dawning of a new day a different cry is heard. Pakak smiles in spite of her sadness at the tired but happy Yuka as she cradles her little son. Pakak believes that Tulok's spirit is now with the newborn, giving her the strength to carry on. She trudges back to her hut to prepare for another day's bone collecting, knowing it is what she must do; to help make the world a safer place for Hanta, the newborn and all the other children to come.

View From the Wire

Linda Sendall

Here we are again, Doris and Derek the pigeons, with our squabs and the rest of our extended family, and believe me there are lots of us just hanging about. We sit high in the trees and watch as you all go past. We notice that everyone has a different gait. Some have heavy bags of shopping, some have buggies and prams with toddlers in tow, some are slow, some are always in a hurry. So many different people.

Today, I see the lady with the pink hair and a walking pole. She has a certain sound, stick one two, stick one two, stick one two. She walks to one side so maybe she has a bad hip. Then she stops to speak to an elderly man who she seems to know. Keeping her distance, she spends a few minutes with him then carries on.

'Food, food, food,' squawks Derek. Off we all fly in a huge flurry of feathers and wings to number thirteen. The lady who lives there always puts on a good spread for us, with no exception today as we have bread, cake, fruit and bird nuts. After our meal we head back to our "wire" to observe the rest of the day as it unfolds.

It's a bit chilly, but there are quite a few people around and the usuals are about to start their day. First to pass is the young lady with a double buggy and a toddler. They walk slow whatever the weather. I feel sorry for her as it is quite a struggle because the buggy and toddler do not all fit on the pavement. So the toddler has to walk behind, quite unaware of the dangers of the traffic that passes. Poor mum is always looking out for the child and today is no exception, but thankfully not much traffic at the moment. They stop as the child's shoe has come off.

Mum is trying to sort that out whilst holding onto the buggy. A man passes by. I sense he wants to help but in this day and age he is unable to, so he rushes past. Shoe on, so onwards to the shop.

Next is the cyclist; not a great fan of those as they take up most of the road and seem to think that social distancing does not apply to them. Why do they wear black? Surely people need to see them. But I think we will always hear them coming as they puff and exhale all the way up the hill.

'Incoming,' squeaks little Pip. It's Eric, fat and round just like his dad. The wire wobbles and bounces as he lands on it.

'News, news,' Eric squawks very loudly. 'There are road works and a new estate as well just up the road. Think of all those workmen with lunch boxes full of sandwiches, cakes and biscuits and maybe even a burger van; we won't have to fly so far anymore,' he said as he flapped his wings making the wire wobble again.

'Chips, chips chips,' cries Derek and off he flies. Some time later he flies back with a big, fat belly full of chips and other scraps he has found. I get the hump with him. He is such a fat bird, soon he will not be able to fly, he will be so heavy; but he won't listen.

'Here come the children,' says one of the squabs. We like them as they always have biscuits and chocolate that they usually drop out of the pushchair, and we are always there to clear up after them. We sit on the wire waiting for them to pass us. Today they have gloves on, which is good for us as they are not able to hold a biscuit; and there it goes, one chocolate biscuit. As we fly down to retrieve it the "adult" bends down, wipes it and shoves it back into the child's hand. We are now in a frenzy. WE need that biscuit. It's our biscuit. We squawk and circle and flap about. The child just laughs so we go back to the wire and sulk.

Next to go by are the people with wheelbarrows obviously on their way to the allotments. They are sometimes good for a bite of something. We position ourselves on the wire just to watch and see what they have got. We have to wait sometime as they decide to chat to passersby. Eventually they get tools out for digging, and digging means worms. They are good to eat but flipping hard work as we have to pull and tug at the worms; may not bother today.

'Quick, quick,' the squawk goes up, 'it's them, quick quick.' We fly back to the wire to be greeted with the sight of the Lycra clad joggers. We always laugh at them. There are a few types; the runner who has always run, has the gear, and arms and legs are coordinated, the professional ones; then there are ones who run in a group. Well, I say run, but they don't. They chat and drink coffee and take up the pavements, not really caring who wants to pass them; then there are the ones who have all the gear, but no idea. They struggle with no coordination whatsoever, but look good in the latest gear and the most expensive trainers that money can buy.

'Where's Derek?' asked Doris.

'He's gone to the M11 as a lorry has shed its load of wheat and it's all over the road,' said one of the squabs. He is so greedy and so fat, good job pigeon pie is not fashionable. He would be perfect.

'They're coming now. Oh look. NO. NO. NO, definitely NO. Some people are just not built for jogging and running.' The birds are laughing so much that they nearly fall off the wire. 'Why don't they look in the mirror before they venture out?'

'No idea,' said Doris, 'but they do try I suppose. Where is Derek? It's dustbin day and he likes the dustcart. It's the highlight of his week. Where is he?'

Derek has left the spilled wheat on the M11, after having eaten most of it, but just as he nears home, he sees the dustcart approaching. Being greedy, he doesn't bother to fly the rest of the way and get the others to share the spoils of the dustcart; he just wants more food. A whole bin has been spilled onto the road. He swoops down, totally forgetting how full and heavy he is now.

He misjudges the distance and splat there he is in all his glory on the front of the dustcart splayed out for all to see.

As the dustcart carried on up the road one of the squabs said, 'Derek has just gone past on the front of the dustcart.'

'Oh well,' replied Doris, 'he won't have to go far for food, will he? Greedy bird.'

Bittersweet - A Paris Interlude

Sally Rich

She looked up in anticipation at the waiter.

'Une tarte et un café, madame.'

'Ah, merci bien.'

She smiled as her eyes took in the beauty of the magnificent tarte; ripe red raspberries shining under their glaze, with the crème pâtissière peeping through, supported by a crisp, honey-coloured pastry. Ah, they always served such lovely pâtisserie in Les Deux Magots.

She carefully cut into the tarte with her fork. Just small mouthfuls these days; swallowing was becoming a bit of a problem. Her hand trembled slightly as she carried the succulent morsel towards her mouth and she dropped a little pale crème onto the skirt of her blue dress. Ah, well. Nobody to notice anyway. Not anymore.

She leant back against the fragile chair and memories of earlier days came flooding into her head. When she had been so beautiful that even Picasso had turned to stare as she drank her evening coffee there. Of course in those days she had not been able to afford the pâtisserie, but she had scraped together enough centimes to sit with one coffee for an hour and enjoy watching the glamorous and famous who met, drank and argued their evenings away in the old café.

Her mind wandered forward to those fraught times during the Nazi occupation. Long days spent in the little workshop near the Palais-Royal. It had seemed unbelievable that people still wanted smart hats with war right on their doorstep. Grateful for the work, although she had wondered if some of the hats so lovingly made were being bought by Nazi officers for their collaborationist mistresses. But there, one had to eat and making hats was all she knew.

Life had not been too difficult at first, but things inevitably became worse. Young and pretty, that should have been an asset, but the problem was so many bored, predatory soldiers patrolling the streets. She took to covering her hair with a scarf and wearing an old and worn coat to hide her figure while scurrying around in the shadows trying to keep out of their way. Her hatred and fear of them had been absolute. How dare they despoil her beautiful Paris, her beautiful France, with their coarse manners and arrogance.

The waiter appeared again.

'Terminée, Madame?'

She nodded, a smile touching the corners of her mouth.

'Encore un café, s'il vous plait.'

Two officers from the Police Nationale strolled past the café, and her thoughts were pushed back to that fateful day of 19th August 1944. Paris had been resounding with rumours. Allied soldiers were coming to save the city; the Nazis would be defeated soon. It was so unsettling; a terrifying time. The police had been on strike for several days and the Germans were very jittery. She had decided that day not to go to work, there was such a strange atmosphere, filled with anticipation; you could almost feel the tension in the air. She scurried along to Les Deux Magots and tucked herself away in a corner seat to sip her coffee. Of course no one could get real coffee, usually just a mix of roasted barley or acorns, but one survived. Several older French men were sitting around drinking and talking in whispers, when suddenly half a dozen men of the Resistance, the Gardiens de la Paix FFI, burst in.

'Monsieur Luizet. Nous cherchons Monsieur Luizet.' Urgency in their voices.

A tall, thin man stood up. Short dark hair, swept back from his forehead, greying at the sides, round-rimmed glasses reflecting the lights of the café. They hurriedly explained. The Prefecture had been taken by the Resistance. Buissière had been arrested. De Gaulle had designated Charles Luizet as the new Prefect of Police. Luizet was wanted straight away at the Prefecture. She looked on in amazement as he hurried away, flanked by his Resistance bodyguards.

Ah, but that was just the beginning. Days of fighting followed and still the Allies did not arrive. The Nazis were arresting people on the smallest excuse and many innocent, and some not so innocent, had been shot. She had remained hidden in her tiny flat, eking out her food. Too scared to venture outside.

Then, on that fateful Thursday night, she heard boots quietly climbing the fire escape. A scratching on her door. She did not answer. More scratching. Someone trying the handle. She opened the door a fraction and a young German soldier rushed in past her. Tousled blonde hair, a wild look in his ice blue eyes. She screamed.

'Please, please, no danger. Close the door. Please, please.' His French was very poor. He was so young, not much older than her and shaking with fear.

'What do you want? I have done nothing. I am only a girl. Please do not hurt me.'

'No, I not hurt. Please, men after me. Please, I not want to die. Hide. Hide.'

She heard rough French voices shouting in the

yard outside.

‘He must be around here somewhere. Nazi bastard.’

‘Please. I not want fight French. I good man. Please. Hide. Hide.’

Tears were running down his smooth cheeks now, hardly any stubble to stop their course, he looked so young. He threw his gun on the floor, his hands in the air.

‘We’ll try all the apartments. He must be holed up somewhere. When I get hold of him – the son of a bitch.’

His companion laughed.

‘Ouais! They’re all a load of dogshit. Wait ‘til we get hold of him! He won’t be seeing his Ma again.’

She looked at the boy with horror.

‘Quick, under my bed. Here, here. Hide your gun too.’ She pushed him right under and made sure the coverlet was down to the floor and quietly pulled the bedroom door closed behind her.

A clatter up the stairs and a thump on the door.

'Hello in there. Open up. We are looking for a bastard Nazi soldier.'

More heavy banging on the door.

She opened it just a crack and peered out.

'What? What are you saying? Nazis here? Where?'

The man pushed against the door and eyed her up and down greedily, his gaze resting on her breasts.

'Sorry, mademoiselle. We are looking for a Nazi soldier.'

'Mon Dieu. Has he done something dreadful? Why do you look here?'

'Dreadful, yes. He's a Nazi. That's dreadful enough for anyone, yes? They know they're beaten. Allies will be here soon. Those British soldiers are soft. They'll only take them prisoner. Me and Armand here, we're going to kill as many as we can before they arrive.'

She looked in horror at the man.

‘I have seen no soldiers, Nazi or otherwise. And your language is very bad. Please go. My mother will be home soon.’

‘Sorry, chérie,’ a parting leer at her neckline. ‘Come on Armand, he’ll be in one of these apartments, or skulking behind the bins. We’ll get him. Vive La France!’

They laughed raucously and ran back down the stairs.

The two of them had waited for hours until it seemed safe for him to crawl out from under the bed. All the time her heart was thumping in her chest. What if they came back? They would kill her too. Or worse!

Finally all around became quiet. She made him barley coffee, thin and weak but all she had, and gave him some stale bread, the only food left in the apartment now.

What to do? He was the enemy, but so young and handsome and scared. Give him up to a brutal death? She could not find it in her heart to do such a thing. So he stayed. On the Friday, the Allied troops had started to enter the city and the sound of street fighting and tanks and guns was everywhere. Still he stayed. She was very frightened; she knew what happened to collaborators. But was she a collaborator? She was a true French woman; but he was just a boy, just a scared boy. They were both so hungry.

On the third night, when the city was quieter, they decided it would be safe for him to venture outside. She made him leave his gun behind and he crept out into the night to surrender to the British soldiers. They both cried when he left. What would happen to him? Would she ever know?

The tears started anew in her old eyes as she thought of him back then. So young, so scared, so beautiful. Dragged into a war that he did not choose for a leader he loathed. The fate of so many young soldiers. She shook her head slowly, side to side, as she thought of all those that died in wars; young men and women, children, so many of them innocent victims of the hatred and hunger for power of the few.

'Your bill, Madame Schmidt. It is so nice that you still come to visit us when you are in Paris. How is your family in Dortmund? All well, I hope?' The old waiter smiled at her.

'I am afraid my husband passed away a few months ago. I came back alone this time because Paris is where I first met him you know.'

Christmas Eve

Marilyn Bromley

She couldn't sleep. It had become a habit, this early morning waking, so she left the house to jog along the cliffside. The cold seemed to invade her soul. As she passed the hilltop houses in darkness, she felt as if she were the only person in the world. It was high tide and the waves smashed on to the rocks below. She took no joy from these solitary moments but she knew once she was at home in the warm shower, she would be glad she had made the effort. It wouldn't last; by the afternoon, she would revert to her normal self.

Rounding the bend, she was taken aback to see a figure on the cliff edge, staring out to sea. The dark figure gave no clue as to whether it was male or female but, as she drew nearer, there was something familiar, something she recognised. Her heart began to beat faster as she passed the figure and could not believe just who it was she was seeing. She veered off to the right, across the grass. Coming to a stop at the road's edge, she stared at the back of the figure, recognising the set of the shoulders, the tip to one side of the head. She was sure this was Annabelle Dart, the woman who had made her life a misery; who had made her lose her job and, far worse, lose her self-esteem and push her over the edge. It had been 15 years since she had last seen Annabelle but there was no mistaking her. All the old feelings bubbled up; the overwhelming feeling of fear and confusion: why was she being like this - why had she been like that?

She stayed and watched her. Still; Annabelle stood, not moving. It was strange to experience all those old feelings, these feelings she had buried for so long. She was still in the moment; and then an even stranger experience overwhelmed her as she found herself running full pelt towards this woman she had not seen for so many years, and with one tremendous push she forced her over the cliff's edge on to the rocks. Her heart was rising in her chest and everything seemed to go silent. She was shocked to find she had not gone over the cliff together with her target; that she was still standing upright, albeit unsteady on her feet.

She did not look over the edge to see where Annabelle had fallen. She did not want to know whether she was dead or alive, but she turned to see if anyone could have witnessed what had happened. Lights were on in the houses now but there was no sign of movement anywhere as she jogged home.

Of course, it was on the lunchtime news and, when she went to the newsagents later that day, she heard people gossiping about it. Annabelle was dead, there was no doubt. The day was interminable.

The following morning, Detective Inspector Goldhawk called. With him was a young girl who looked as if she could be his granddaughter but, apparently, according to her uniform, was a police constable. DI Goldhawk was a man of few words and certainly no niceties.

‘We have information you were on the clifftop at crack of dawn yesterday morning, around 6:30. Can you tell me what you saw?’

‘Nothing. There was no one about.’

‘We understand you knew Annabelle Dart. You were colleagues at the medical centre?’

‘Yes, that’s right. We worked together for several years.’

‘Friends?’

‘Not friends exactly. Work colleagues.’

‘Hmm’ he paused, ‘we are given to understand there was some animosity between you.’

‘Not really. She found fault with some of my work. She may have been right. I don’t know. I was not well at the time.’

‘Hmm.’ DI Goldhawk ‘Hmm’d’ a lot. The young girl looked embarrassed and gave her a sympathetic look as they left.

She moved about the house slowly for the rest of the day. There was no rest. So they thought it was murder, not an accident? The word ‘murder’ had not occurred to her until now. She had murdered. It sounded odd; that word seemed to have nothing to do with her. But then her mind wandered to the thought of who could have seen her.

There was no one on the clifftop that morning and not even a single car passed. Then she remembered: Olive! Olive had worked with them at the medical centre and her chalet bungalow faced the sea. She had bought it especially for the sea view from the upstairs bedroom. Always a gossip, Olive, and she would happily approach the police, without being asked, just to get in on the act. It was Olive who, when Annabelle was being particularly unpleasant, had said, 'that is tantamount to bullying'. But she had not mentioned it to the manager. No one had. No one had stood up for her; putting their own best interests before her own. It was understandable but where was the British sense of fairness?

After she had lost her job, she lost her marriage. He walked out the day after she told him she had walked out of her job.

'But I'm ill,' she said.

'You're not ill,' he said, 'You're bloody mental!' And so she had moved into the tiny cottage on the edge of town, where she could see the sea. He was right after all. She was mental - mentally ill. No one could do what she had done unless they were completely and utterly deranged. She would never leave the house again. How could she?

Two days later, the telephone rang. It was thc young girl, the 'granddaughter'. She sounded as if she had never made a professional 'phone call before. 'We won't be making any further enquiries.'

'What does that mean?' she asked, hardly daring to breathe.

'I can't say exactly but we won't need to speak to you again. New evidence has come to light.' It sounded as if the girl was being prompted.

So she did leave the house. It was cold and grey, looking as if it might snow, but there were festive lights everywhere, although she hardly registered them. As she entered the newsagents, someone brushed past her. He looked back and then stopped.

'Hello, Amanda isn't it?' It was Jim, Annabelle's husband. He looked drawn.

'Jim, what on earth are you doing out and about?'

'Couldn't bear the thought of Annabelle's face on the front of the local paper, so I bought the lot.' There was no sign of the papers.

'On no,' he said, noting that she was looking for evidence. 'I didn't want them. The manager was very nice. I paid him to take them off the shelf.'

'I'm so sorry,' she said, trying to sound calm.

'It's ok, Amanda. I may as well tell you, you'll hear soon enough.' He paused and took a breath. They were blocking the doorway, so Jim guided her on to the pavement. 'Don't know whether you or the others at work were aware, but Annabelle was ill. I thought it was her time of life but no, she was never quite right. And, latterly, she was haunted by something in the past. I found the note in my shed. Said she couldn't forgive herself.'

Amanda made her way home. It all made sense. The lack of resistance; almost like she was politely giving in to what was happening; the ease with which she tumbled over the cliff, not even making a sound. No cry for help.

People she vaguely knew called greetings to her but she did not hear them. As she opened the front door, the 'phone rang.

'Hello Mum. Hope you're ready. Have you got the tree up? I'm picking Jack up tomorrow at eleven but he probably won't be ready.'

Amanda could not speak.

'Are you alright Mum?'

It was Christmas Eve.

After the Twa Corbies - A Medieval Mystery

Allan James

Willum perched at the bar, watched as a family of pony trekkers sloshed their way into the public bar of The King's Bint, picked up his almost full half pint of Old Monk and took a minute sip. He placed the glass carefully on the bar then burst into a fit of deep, chesty coughing. He hawked up a lump of something and tongued it into the filthy rag he kept in his pocket for such events.

Behind the bar Bethany, the landlord's beautiful daughter, polished glasses and wondered how busy she'd be later.

I, as usual, sat in the corner unseen by them all. I knew that Willum was waiting for the pony trekkers to come back downstairs, and I knew they'd visit the bar for a drink after their meal. Bethany had a casual approach to kids being in the bar. There wasn't anywhere else for them to go and as long as they were with their parents things were ok, and Bill Proctor, the local constable, wasn't bothered as long as they didn't serve alcohol to the kids.

Up in their connected rooms I could hear the mother, an excitable Italian woman, protest to her husband that this wasn't the time for that. I could have shifted my attention to see just what she meant, but I could guess. I'd been around for so long now that nothing came as much of a surprise. In fact, for donkey's years, nothing had happened in the parish that I hadn't seen or heard. That was one of the advantages of having been here that long; not only did I know the history, I was part of it and I'd been here to see the rest. After a while the fun wore off and eventually you just wanted it to end, at least I did.

Upstairs, the Italian woman stepped naked out of the shower, slapped her husband's hands away and told him she meant it when she said not now.

Downstairs in the bar, the door opened and the butcher came in, followed by his wife and their dog. A nasty little terrier of some kind that didn't like me and growled whenever I moved. I usually did this when Willum had reached a crucial point in his story and, because the dog always growled, listeners invariably thought it must mean something. And if I stood up the dog went mad; barking and scrabbling at the cracked tiles on the floor and straining to get at the seat beside the fire. It always impressed. The funny thing is none of the locals, and certainly not Willum, even knew I was there; they just thought the dog was stupid.

I turned my concentration back to the bar; the Italian woman came downstairs and went, with her wet haired kids and sheepish husband, into the dining room; the butcher ordered another drink for him and his wife, the dog settled down, growled a couple of times when I moved in my seat and Bethany polished a few more glasses. The outer door opened and Bill Proctor lumbered in and ordered his pint.

About an hour later the Italian mama's family came back from the dining room and eyed up the table beside the fire. I could tell they were going to settle there so I moved away. The kids had a squabble over who would sit where to face the rest of the room. Their mother went to sit on the chair I'd just left. She sat. She shivered. She got up and took the complaining children with her to another table saying it was strange that on such a warm evening it should be so very cold in the corner.

Old Willum of course could tell them why. 'That's cos o' the ghost,' he said nudging his half empty glass. The Italian woman's husband looked at him and Willum, never slow to take advantage of someone's hesitation, coughed again before adding, 'that'd be Sir Godwin' he curled his hand round his glass, ''im what was killt, mysterious like. Years back it were.'

The husband was interested. 'Who's Godwin?' he asked, 'the lord of the manor?' He grinned at Willum, 'so when was this, back with the Victorians?'

'Nah,' Willum said, beginning to turn his back but still managing to push his glass an inch or two towards the husband, 'long afore that.'

In the end of course, the husband's curiosity gets the better of him. A drink was bought for Willum who quickly downed the remains of his half pint and took a quick slurp of his new drink before he settled himself on the stool to begin his tale. The story of the knight Godwin, who was killed, and his wife who went missing. And his hawk, and his hound, who were left to their own devices. And, according to Willum, the only witnesses were the two ravens that sat in the tree and watched the crime unfold. It was a mystery that the village bailiff never did solve.

'Tis a famous folk song,' said Willum, 'how the knight got 'imself killt and his wife was took by some other fellow.' And he went on to tell how the remains of the body was found the next spring behind an old field wall. His wife, his hounds and his hawk had long gone and there was no answer to the mystery.

Willum, now at the end of his pint, paused and hinted that there was more. The Italian woman, excited by the thought of more, gave her husband the look that said, if you want what I promised, you'd better buy him another drink. The drink was bought, along with another pint for himself, a glass of house white for her, and two colas for the kids.

'Well,' Willum continued, 'what was bailiff t'think?' He took another loud slurp from his glass and told them that he thought there were two possibilities. One was that the woman had been abducted and that a ransom was due, but the husband had chased after her and her kidnapper and had caught them up on the moor, only to be killed and dumped in a ditch. 'Trouble is,' said Willum, 'if that'd happened, where was her body?' He explained that if she was taken for ransom and the husband had caught them and been killed, then what was the point of keeping her? The villain wouldn't have got a penny for her, so even if he'd had his way with her, he wouldn't have kept her. So, either she escaped, in which case where did she go; or he killed her, but where was her body? Willum's other theory, after a rueful look at his near empty glass, was that she had gone off with this other fellow, her lover, but her husband had realised, had caught up with them, and had been killed and she'd carried on to a new life with her new man.

What Willum couldn't say of course was what really happened. He couldn't say because he wasn't there nor could he make it up because even he didn't have enough imagination. In reality, events are often far more exaggerated than in fiction. Sir Godwin was killed. I know because I did it. We were travelling on foot, up the valley and through the pass that led to the neighbouring village and the road that led to the sea. He had charged up behind us, leapt off his horse and fallen, hauberk first, on top of me and winded himself. His wife had picked up a rock and hit him on top of his head, denting the helmet he wore. I staggered to my feet, drew my dagger and drove it upward into his throat through the unprotected area below his chin. We thought he was dead so we dragged his body to the stone wall, stood him against it and toppled him over, into the ditch in the neighbouring parish. Then we rode away into what I thought would be a magnificent sunset.

We continued on our way until we reached this village and this inn. Pretending to be travellers who had lost their way, we took a room for the night. She was upset and we argued. We fought, I was injured, she killed me and fled into the night. And now I'm here, unshriven and trapped in this village; or more accurately, within the parish boundary.

So Willum is right, the corner by the fire does have a ghost, but not Sir Godwin, it's me. And before you ask, I've no idea where his ghost might be, only that he didn't die in this parish.

So This Is Christmas

Elizabeth Jennings

First it was Christmas jumper day, then a party, then Christmas Eve and Christmas Day. 'What shall we dress the baby in?' seemed to be the constant question. On reflection, Christmas jumper day was the best. They'd managed to find a little top with a cute penguin on the front and a matching hat. Well, I suppose it wasn't too bad, although the tights could've been smaller. I couldn't crawl without catching them and bumping my nose on the floor, but they tucked them underneath me in the pushchair.

The party. Don't even go there! You want to know? OK. The family had sent out the teenager (my big brother) to find another cute outfit for the baby. Eek, I could not believe my eyes! Whatever possesses anyone to make a reindeer outfit for a baby? Of course, there were antlers to finish the whole thing off nicely – with bells on the end of each branch which made a hideous jingle. These antlers were attached to a sort of bonnet which had a bright red nose on the front of it. I could hardly see. Also, it seemed my brother and sister got great amusement from pulling on the antlers to set them off; jingle, jangle – oh, please, not again. When we got to the party, which was about my bedtime, I decided I would just scream so they'd have to take me home. Didn't work.

Hundreds, well I might be exaggerating a bit, maybe just some, big people kept poking at me, smiling and saying such stupid things as: 'Did the little reindeer want something to eat?' 'Are we being a party pooper here?' and then laughing. I'll give them something to laugh at – I know what poop is. Several explosions later I was taken off to the bathroom. I had exceeded myself. Right through the whole outfit. Had to be stripped and wrapped in a towel. Ha! That did the trick, no one came anywhere near me, I was put in my pram and left to my own devices, by which time I was so tired I nodded off. Bet it spoilt their party though. I won't be invited back until I have an adult reindeer costume.

Christmas Eve. The neighbours' kids came to help decorate an enormous green tree. I was put in my chair so I could watch the fun. Brahms, the family tortoiseshell cat, wanted to assist by jumping at each ornament once it was tied on. I giggled.

'Oh, look at the baby – he's really enjoying this,' said one small girl. She advanced towards me, stretching out her arms.

'Can I pick him up?' and without waiting for a reply she attached me to her, dragging me across the floor just as my mother shouted:

'Put him down!' in such a loud voice that she dropped me.

As my head hit the floor I screamed, clenching my fists and pulling up my legs. Do they think I'm a

TOY? Clearly they do as when my mother picked me up and cuddled me, 'Oh, he hasn't got a Christmas outfit on, did we get one for today?'

Within minutes I was being undressed and then metamorphosed (is that a real word?) as an Elf – vivid green, yet another bell on my hat, and an inbuilt fat tummy. Immediately a hideous child nearly strangled me by tying tinsel round my neck. I reached out and managed to bop her on the nose, making her cry out. Serves her right.

At teatime, the mums and dads came to collect their little darlings and were invited to stay for a drink. One of the mums approached me, deciding she'd help by putting a spoonful of gloop into my mouth. I tried clamping my mouth shut, but she forced it open by pushing the spoon against my gums whilst making a choo-chooing noise. Goodness knows what that was! Anyway I had this mouthful of said gloop so I thought I'd try the 'blowing a raspberry trick'. Well, that showed her! She'll never try to feed me again. All down the front of her blouse it was. Very satisfying.

Another lady decided I needed to have a cuddle. She dragged me out of my highchair, nearly catching one of my feet in the harness, wiped round my mouth with a dishcloth (yuk) then she bounced me around, made me burp and then asked if Santa was bringing me something special. No idea what she was talking about but I smiled winsomely which seemed to please her. I was put to bed being told to watch out for Father Christmas – what? Not worth worrying about I thought as I dropped off to sleep.

Christmas Day. At breakfast, as well as my usual scrambled egg, big sister Chloe tried to force-feed me something orange. It was slimy so I spat it out. As it landed on the floor, Liszt, our other cat, pounced on it and ran out of the room, with my sister following her at speed.

'Give me back my smoked salmon,' she shouted.

After breakfast the big parcels under the tree were handed out. I was given a piece of bright paper to tear at, which I did, putting some of it in my mouth – not very tasty. A rattling toy which is bright red and yellow. I shake it. Everyone smiles at me and gives me another piece of paper to rip apart. Inside was what looked like something to wear. Uh oh, something to wear? Yep, you've probably guessed that it is yet another Christmas outfit. Oh my goodness . . . . . I thought the reindeer was bad enough. The rest of the family is watching me, all squealing with delight, as I pull out a loopy babygro sort of thing with a hood attached.

'A sheep!' squeals Chloe 'Let me put it on him.'

I'm stripped half naked and pushed into this all-in-one fluffy suit, again which is clearly made for a baby twice my size. My mother buttons me into it, pulls up the hood, which flops over my eyes and then lifts me up so I can see myself in the hall mirror. The EARS are nearly as big as my head and, as she pulls the hood up from over my eyes, I can just see another pair of eyes above them. Horror of horrors! I'm then carefully put on the floor to crawl around whilst everyone laughs and makes a sort of 'baa' sound. Next thing I know I am being chased by two cats, one of them pulling at my 'ear' and the other jumping at my 'tail'. I roll over and scream – works every time. Brahms and Liszt are chased out and the children told to keep them away whilst my mother hugs me.

Throughout the day everyone seems to be eating. There's a lovely smell coming from the kitchen and then what looks like a big bird is put on the table with lots of other things and a bit of everything is put in front of me. Some of it nice, some, especially the green things, more worthy of spitting out or throwing under the table at the cats. Later the family play games whilst I watch from my chair and then it seems there is more food. I'm given something fruity and then something sweet in a bowl with custard, followed by Chloe feeding me her sweets. These are really nice so I stretch out my hands for more. Now I may have a lot of words in my head but I can't actually speak many of them but 'more' is one I use a lot to good effect. Suddenly I'm not feeling quite so well. I cry a bit, looking for my mother but daddy picks me up and throws me up in the air (this is one of his games). He probably shouldn't have done that. A moment later almost my entire day's food is carefully deposited all over his head.

'Mother!' he shouts 'Come and get the baby – he's just turned me into a multicolour sick bucket.'

‘Oh, poor darling, come here,’ she says, taking me from him. ‘I expect he’s overexcited with all the fun. I’ll get him to bed. Come on Sweetie Pie!’

She takes me upstairs, undresses me, washes me, puts me in clean nightclothes, holds me in the air and gives me a lovely kiss, cuddles me, and as she puts me into my cot says, ‘What did you think of your first Christmas then? Wasn’t it lovely? Only another week and we’ll be celebrating New Year. We can’t keep you up for the fireworks, but we’ve got you the cutest little outfit for the afternoon. Everyone will love you in it, you’ll look so, ooh, yummy.’

I curled up, put my thumb in my mouth and as my eyelids are growing heavy, I’m thinking ‘I can hardly wait!’

Visiting St Peter

Lavinia Epworth

All I can say to you is I am not ready. I know that I look dreadful. This hospital gown does nothing for me, I've never been able to wear off white, and I haven't slept for days. It's no wonder, hospital wards are not unlike the hard shoulder on the M11 for the amount of traffic whizzing by and the volume of noise. So please go away and communicate that to St. Peter's management team. After all I didn't invite you to appear here by my bed looking saintly.

Ok I know that you have quotas to fulfil but take

her in the next bed, her groaning is driving me crazy. When she's not groaning she's snoring. What a waste of space, not to mention she's taking up a valuable NHS bed. Even you must have heard about the dire state of the NHS. If you ask me you need to be a lot more efficient and responsible in your choices. If I was your boss, Peter Saint whatever he calls himself, I would be considering another post for you; let's face it you are pretty rubbish at this one. Where were you when I longed to enter your pearly gates six months ago? I would have welcomed you then. God knows I took enough tablets to make it happen, not the el cheapos from Tesco's either, these were the proper Paracetamols from Boots, although I did add some of Mum's pain killers, she gets them on prescription so doesn't have to pay. Admittedly I was stupid to choose the graveyard as my last resting place on that occasion. Somehow I wanted to be near dad and leaning against his gravestone seemed reassuring, God knows it was the only time I've had any support from him! However, my plan was foiled on that occasion. Who knew so many people 'rocked up' to church on a Sunday? I tell you I was almost blinded by the glow of their halos as they rescued me from the clutches of death. What a carry on. I bet there were extra hallelujahs in church that Sunday. Anyway, I digress. You asked me how I got here; there again you should have this information already.

It all started when Shirley asked me if I would join the Escort agency. She'd been working for them for a while and some of the tales she tells are unbelievable. However, even in school she told 'porkies' and was often regaled with 'Liar, liar your pants on fire'. At the time I was skint due to circumstances beyond my control, mainly wrongful dismissal. OK I can see that look on your face. Maybe some of my past you already know. Let's put it this way, I didn't know there were cameras in the stationery cupboard.

At my Escort interview I was told that an escort was just that. You are taken to high class establishments by respectable gentlemen who are usually lonely and loaded; definitely no 'extras' expected. I did wonder later whether being requested to cover the man in shaving foam from bald head to flabby butt could be counted as going above and beyond my remit. The extra £200 he gave me probably answered that uncertainty. I hoped that he left a generous tip for the poor woman from the Philippines who had to clean the room after he left. It's surprising how much foam is in each can and he had three. After that I had so many appointments where all I had to do was listen to the client, admittedly not all interesting, but the compensation for the boredom was that my Tesco's grocery bill was halved because of the dinners I was treated to; so cooking dinner was a thing of the past. Result!

My last assignment came with a list of instructions. Shirley said that this was not unusual, and I would be paid for the items on the list by the agency. One of the purchases was Dior perfume, Diorissimo to be exact. I made sure that I bought the real stuff, no 'eau de bog' for me. I reckoned that if I had to spend time shopping when I could be watching Eastenders, there had to be compensation. The dress that I had to buy was neither my colour nor my style, but I would give it to my sister. I knew she would like it. Giving her a suitable explanation as to its origin could be problematic but I would be advised by

Shirley, the life-long liar.

Freshly showered, perfumed, hair up, dress on, six-inch-high heels clacking, I journeyed into Liverpool Street Station, turned left then left again, to catch the taxi at a place that not many people know about; no being accosted by the fumes from McDonald's for me. I was hot to trot and I knew it. As the cab drove through Oxford Street I was aware of the women in hijabs and felt a stab of pity and anger. Alright I was being bought by a man, but for most of my life I had the choice to be me, whereas I suspect those women did as they were told. A bit like you're trying to do with me now and I am still not ready, so settle down there's more to tell.

I arrived at the Churchill, Portman Square, passing by Selfridges and for once in my life realising that those goods were now available to me, whereas in the past I would not have even contemplated going in. I was not a hooker; no, I was an escort. I felt a small glow of pride. My diary was full and so was my purse. I had been able to put money aside for my daughter and even take out a life insurance policy, just in case. The reception was plush, large, and impersonal. I wondered if Mr Hassan had done this before. He had certainly chosen carefully. I was greeted by his Personal Assistant and we glided up to the Royal Suite, a large, sumptuous apartment with several bedrooms and a dining room. I was instructed to enter, make myself comfortable and await the arrival of my client. Half an hour later a young sweat-soaked individual entered from the Fitness Suite, looked me up and down nodding approvingly. He then went to shower. It reminded me of the film Pretty Woman. I've always fancied Richard Geere.

The evening was centred around a business dinner served in the dining room. There would be eight guests and my instructions were to sit, say nothing, and look interested. I was obviously window dressing. I noted that even the floral displays matched the colour of my dress exactly. Before the guests arrived, I was adorned by Mr Hassan's PA. A magnificent diamond necklace with matching bracelet and earrings were placed on me with great care and adjusted to perfection. I tell you I felt royal. The dinner was conducted in a language that I did not understand so there was no chance of me putting my foot in it in English. I think it went well. I was constantly admired, or was it the jewels, who knows? Dinner over, Mr Hassan escorted his guests downstairs. I awaited further instructions but, before that could happen, I received a sharp blow on the head and in a semi-conscious state was roughly bundled into a laundry basket and then into the boot of a car. Sometime later I awoke in hospital, jewels gone, half conscious, head bandaged and a splitting headache. How I got here I have no idea. You, unfortunately, are my first visitor and I know that visiting time is over so why aren't the nurses chucking you out? It's almost like you're invisible.

I know the prognosis is not good otherwise you would not keep pestering me to go with you. Mentioning meeting up with St. Peter is not doing it for me but I believe he has awesome gates. Will I be admitted? Well, that is another matter. Heaven for me is here, walking in Hatfield Forest with my dog and daughter, having a laugh with Shirley, even seeing who's the next to depart this life in Eastenders. Maybe after Shirley has been and I've explained what happened to me I'll take a stroll with you and meet the old codger. I don't want to leave this earthly coil with suspicion as to the whereabouts of the jewels hanging over me; that's not fair to my little girl. Then there's the insurance to think about. It's gone very quiet in here, have you reeled in that noisy nuisance in the next bed? Thank God for that. A good night's sleep for me at last and a fulfilled quota for you. Job Done.

Maud's Legacy

Marilyn Bromley

September 2013

Elizabeth turned the key in the lock and opened the door to her mother's home. The air was still and cold.

'It smells,' said Lucy.

'It's just musty,' said her mother. 'It's been empty for a few weeks. I just couldn't face doing this before.' They moved into the bedroom and opened the wardrobe door.

‘Nan had a lot of clothes,’ sighed Lucy. ‘And yet she wore the same few things all the time.’

‘After Grandad died, she hardly ever went out again and she saved most of her clothes for best; and there never was any best.’ Elizabeth indicated quotation marks round the word best.

‘I’m never going to do that,’ said Lucy. ‘I’m going to wear all my clothes, all the time. And I’m not going to let you be like Nan either.’

‘Hmmm.’

The two women worked silently, making piles of clothes – some for the charity shop, some that Elizabeth would keep and some that Lucy had given her grandmother and wanted to keep in remembrance. When they had finished all the clothes on the hangers, they turned their attention to the shoes in the bottom of the wardrobe. Lucy reached into the back.

‘There’s something in the back here’ she said stretching into the dark recesses. She pulled out a brown leather bag, with a flap.

‘Oh!’ Elizabeth exclaimed. ‘It’s Great Aunt Maud’s sheet music case.’

'It smells,' Lucy said sniffing the leather.

'It's leather, and anyway you say everything smells! It must be over a hundred years old, so what do you expect? You should keep it as an heirloom.'

'No thanks, it will just clutter up the place.'

'Why don't you want anything that has a history?' Elizabeth was exasperated. 'When I was getting married, I was glad of anything anyone offered and I wanted things that meant something to me. You wouldn't even take your great grandmother's tea-set.'

'Nah, we're moving into a modern flat Mum. We don't want your old stuff; it doesn't mean anything to me and it wouldn't look right. These jumpers and scarves I gave Nan are quite enough. Anyway, why did Auntie Maud have a music case?' Lucy could not reconcile the thought of Aunt Maud being a musician with the old lady she could just about remember, sitting in an armchair, looking – not disapproving – but disinterested in life.

'She was a concert pianist when she was young but, when she married Uncle Ernest, she gave it up to be a housewife. It was expected in those days.'

‘Exactly!’ said Lucy. ‘I don’t want to be associated with the repression of women. Give it to a charity shop.’

Elizabeth sighed and gathered up the piles of clothes and all the shoes, stuffing them into carrier bags. They opened the back door and left the house for the last time.

September 2023

Lucy turned the key in the lock and entered her mother’s house. The air was still and cold. She shifted the little girl onto her hip and made her way through to the bedroom.

Plonking her daughter down on the carpet, she opened the wardrobe door. She worked quickly, knowing Tabitha would start crawling all over the place soon enough and she wanted to get this done before there were any catastrophes. So many clothes and most not worn for years. She felt tearful as she saw the garments her mother had worn on special occasions. Her death had been sudden and her perfume still lingered on sweaters and blouses; she was almost still in the room.

When she had finished with the clothes on hangers, making a pile for the charity shop and a pile of things she could not bear to discard, she sorted through the shoes and then moved to the chest of drawers. Tabitha had been quite happy chewing on the rusk Lucy had pressed into her sticky little 'paw' but now, somehow, she had crawled into the bottom of the wardrobe and was tugging at something at the back.

'No, no, no! Tabitha, come out!'

There was much screeching as Lucy pulled the child out of the cupboard. She was clutching something - something that Lucy recognised. It was Great Aunt Maud's music case, looking slightly more battered than the last time she had seen it, but recognisable all the same. Her mother had kept it! Tabitha hung on to it, sniffing it and saying ''bitha's, 'bitha's'.

'Oh come on', said Lucy, trying to wrestle it away from her. 'You don't want that smelly old thing.' But Tabitha persisted and started to wail, ''bitha's'.

'Oh alright, have it your own way.' Lucy put her

down on the floor and gathered up the carrier bags, then manoeuvred Tabitha back on to her hip (more difficult now with the addition of the bags of clothes) and made her way to the front door. Then she stopped, put down the carriers and perched Tabitha on the draining board.

‘Just let me have a look,’ she muttered. After much protest from the child, she managed to open the case. On the inside of the flap was a name and address: Maud Fleet, 43 Rosslyn Court, Hampstead. Tears prickled Lucy’s eyes. Evidence of a life lived and a life thwarted.

‘Ok Tabs, you can keep it. This is your Great, Great Aunt Maud’s.’ Tabitha just sniffed it again.

Lucy opened the back door, turned the key in the lock and left her mother’s house for the last time.

Something To Do

Linda Sendall

A day to myself at last and I have a list of ‘things to do’. I love a things to do list. Maybe it’s the satisfaction of ticking all the jobs off or just having the time to do them all, anyway I have one.

Have to say I am a bit late getting up as my shopping is due to be delivered between seven and eight. It’s now six thirty and I am not ready for it. The fridge needs cleaning out before it gets re-filled so I need to get dressed - but no time, anyway nobody is going to see me so why bother, so I don’t.

I gather cleaning stuff; think I need a wee but that can wait, it's not urgent. Not much in the fridge so won't take many minutes, but I find a tray of blueberries, so put them on the side to have later. Nothing has died in the fridge so a quick clean and done, but as I get up, I catch the sleeve of my dressing gown on the corner of the worktop, which in turn makes me knock over the whole tray of blueberries. Oh boy can blueberries travel; they are all over the place. Unfortunately, I have a black carpet in the kitchen so can't see where they are. If I move, the chances are I will tread them in but on the other hand I can't stand here all day, and I still need a wee. So, what do I do? Such a dilemma. Whatever, I need to be quick as my shopping will arrive very soon.

Right, decision made; pick up what I can see, which is a tidy few. So, I busy myself using the tea towel and a tablespoon to shovel them up. I can't kneel down at the moment due to a knee operation but I think I have managed to get most of them. A few are squashed into the carpet, but will sort that out later. I need a wee. The phone rings at seven fifteen; it's my friend Wendy who can talk for England. I could sort out my shopping and she would still be talking, not even knowing that I wasn't there (we all know someone like that).

'Hi ya,' she says, 'how are you?' and even before I answer she starts. Now I have time for a much needed wee, so I put the phone down with the intention of rushing to the loo but find I've trodden blueberries into my new carpet. I am mortified as I will have to clean it immediately so there are no stains. I find something in the shed that will do. I mutter to myself, 'must have a wee when I have sorted these stains out'. So there I am, sort of kneeling and bending, scrubbing the carpet like a demon, but it's worked. I stand to admire my work only to find that the berries are still stuck to my slipper and have been trodden all through the rest of the house. To say I am mortified is an understatement.

Where is the shopping? He is late. It must be traffic or weather and they usually ring. OMG, Wendy is still on the phone. I pick up the phone to apologise, but she is still talking and I don't think she's even noticed that I have not been there. Go and have a wee NOW. But just as I am about to open the bathroom door, the doorbell rings. 'Timing,' I murmur, 'the shopping at last.' But, no it's some suited blokes with brief cases. I sussed who they are as they have the statutory kid in a pushchair with them. How dare they come here at eight in the morning. I NEED A WEE. On my front gate I have a sign saying "no sellers or religious groups" so I suggest to them that they go and read it and shut the door with a bang.

Would you believe my mobile phone is ringing now. It's my husband saying the delivery man had rung him as my home phone was constantly engaged. Oh, I had forgotten Wendy, so I rush to the phone and she's STILL talking. Then she ends the call quite abruptly as HER shopping had arrived. She said it had been a lovely chat and put the phone down. So, no idea of how she is and I never said a word, but after 45 mins on the phone I assume she is ok.

Now a wee at last but hubby is still on the mobile saying that the shopping is going to be late due to roadworks and road closures. No surprise there. At last I can get my wee, but as time had moved on I needed a little more than a wee. Just as I get to the loo the doorbell goes again. I steel myself to open it to find a man and a woman, very well dressed, polished shoes that you can see your face in. Her make-up is perfect and together with the designer handbag they look as though they have stepped out of a catalogue.

'Surprise,' they shouted. Well it is a surprise as I have no idea who they are, 'We are on our way to the airport and thought we'd call in and take you for breakfast.'

I looked at them blankly as I still had no idea who they were as I stood there in my pjs, a tatty dressing gown with the pocket hanging off and my favourite slippers that have seen better days.

'You don't remember us do you?' she screeched at me.

'Well er.... no to be honest I don't.'

'Oh Brenda, you are still funny. You worked for us....'

'Let me stop you there,' I said, 'I am Denise not Brenda.'

'Oooh Dave,' she said, 'I think we've made a

mistake. Is this 13 New Field Crescent?'

'No it's not. I have something urgent to do so must go.' I hear them apologising but I have no time. As I am closing the door I see the delivery man just pulling up. He usually takes at least 10 minutes to sort it all out, so I hurry to the loo and just as I sit down the doorbell rings. I shout to just leave it on the doorstep.

'No can do,' he shouts back.

'Well give me a minute then.'

'I'm running late,' he shouts again, 'need to get going.'

'Just leave it. I have something to do in a hurry too, so JUST LEAVE IT.'

Meeting the Neighbours

Yvonne Ayres

A loud cry woke Steve from a deep sleep. He had hoped for a lie-in, having arrived home so late last night, but his wife obviously needed help. Rubbing the sleep from his eyes he reluctantly threw back the duvet and sat on the edge of the bed.

'What's up Em?' he called as he searched for his specs.

'Look what they've done. It's vandalism.' Steve sighed. He didn't need to ask who she was talking about. She'd become almost obsessive over what their new neighbours were up to. Their holiday had not had the desired effect of making her a little more relaxed about whatever was going on next door. Bracing himself, he flung a comforting arm around Emma's shoulders and peered through the window to see what had upset her so much. Their car was parked in the drive, the shared front garden wall was intact and apart from their lawn needing a cut he couldn't immediately identify what Emma was so uptight about. He scratched his head saying,

'All looks ok to me. What's the problem?'

'It's the hedge. Reg's prized beech hedge. It's gone.' Looking beyond the lawn Steve finally saw. While they'd been away, the neighbours they had yet to meet had chopped down the magnificent beech hedge that once separated the two driveways.

'Oh Em. I'm sorry. I know how much you loved that hedge.'

'It was Reg's pride and joy.' Emma said tearfully. 'I helped look after it when he went away on holidays and took over when he got too ill to do the gardening. It's all that was left of him. They've completely gutted the house since they moved in, dug up all the mature shrubs, even filled in his beloved pond. Reg will be turning in his grave.'

Steve tightened his arms around his distraught wife. They both missed their old neighbour of over 20 years. Reg had been a surrogate grandfather to their two children as they grew up. Emma had shared his love of gardening, and many a pot of tea, during long winter afternoons while they discussed planting schemes for the next year; whilst he and Reg were both cricket fans supporting the local village team and travelling to watch the odd county game together.

Emma sniffed. 'Putting up with all that drilling, banging and loud music from the workmen during the building work was bad enough but this is the last straw. I'm going round right now to give them a piece of my mind. We can't let them get away with it Scot free.' She pulled away from her husband and marched off to the bathroom.

'Not sure that's a good idea Em. Not while you're so upset. At least wait until you've had some breakfast,' pleaded Steve as he followed her. She closed the bathroom door firmly in his face. He tried again. 'Be reasonable love. It's only 7.30. They might still be in bed,' he pointed out in a last attempt to delay her. Not even stopping to reply, his stoney-faced wife returned to the bedroom, scooped up yesterday's clothes from the floor and silently dressed. Steve recognised the determined look on her angry face and decided to tag along, if only to stop Emma from doing or saying anything she might later regret.

Hopping down the drive with one trainer on and the other in his hand, he hurried to catch up with Emma who was striding ahead. She only paused when she reached the new sleek front door. With no sign of a doorbell she hammered on the wood with her tight fist, and waited. A breathless Steve arrived just as the door was opening. A pair of tired, brown eyes appeared in the narrow gap between the door and the frame.

'Yes?' whispered the owner of the eyes.

Before Emma could say anything, her husband butted in saying, 'sorry it's obviously too early. We'll come back at a more convenient ti…. .'

'Emma and Steve from next door,' his wife loudly interrupted in her no-nonsense ex-teacher's voice. 'May we come in for a moment?' The door slowly opened a little wider revealing a man wearing a skimpy bathrobe that looked far too small for him.

'Yes, of course please come in,' he whispered. 'Would you mind being very quiet. Bad night,' he added with a rueful smile. They followed their host into what used to be a rather poky kitchen in Reg's time, now a roomy, light-filled kitchen diner. The early morning sunshine dazzled through newly installed sky lights, bouncing off the sparkly worktop of the central island unit. To Steve's relief the sight seemed to have robbed his wife of speech; she'd always hankered after an island unit.

'Would you like a tea or a coffee?' The man's quiet voice broke the awe inspired silence. Steve answered for them both, requesting two coffees.

'Oh good you've got the kettle on. I could murder a cup of coffee.' The woman gliding towards them with a wide, warm smile was of statuesque build, accentuated by the voluminous kaftan she wore, topped by a mass of tight black curls. 'You must be our neighbours. Sorry we haven't had time to come round and introduce ourselves, but things have been a little chaotic. I'm Princess and this is my husband, Winston.' As she spoke Princess gave both Emma and Steve a brief but firm handshake. 'Go and take off that silly robe Winston. You look quite ridiculous,' she said with an affectionate smile. Rolling her eyes at her visitors she added, 'I don't know why he's wearing that. Probably the first thing to hand. We did have rather a sleepless night. Anyway, while the coffee's brewing I'll show you around the house. I expect you'd like to see what all the noise has been about.'

Steve held his breath, expecting a furious blast from Emma concerning all the banging and drilling they'd recently had to endure. But Emma seemed completely mesmerised. Wordless, she meekly followed her neighbour, with Steve close behind. They were soon marvelling over the difference knocking down a wall and building a small extension onto the back had made. There was still some decorating to do but it would look amazing once finished. Upstairs a guest bedroom with ensuite had been created in the two-storey extension. Peeking through the door of the original back bedroom, Emma and Steve were totally gobsmacked to see two tiny babies sleeping in cribs placed close together.

'That's what's kept us too busy for visiting,' explained their hostess in a low voice. 'Born prematurely just as we were about to move in; they've only just been discharged from hospital.'

'So what do you think of our new neighbours now?' asked Steve as he and Emma sat down to breakfast an hour later back at home.

'Well, I can see why they haven't been around much what with having to go to and from the hospital. Weren't the babies gorgeous?'

'Not getting broody, I hope?' teased Steve. 'What did you think of the house?'

'Beautiful. Very modern. But did you notice they'd left Reg's old kitchen tiles on the wall in the new utility room? Thought that was a nice touch.' Emma paused, remembering how Princess had talked almost affectionately about Reg, having learnt all about him from Reg's daughter whilst buying the house.

Staring out the window she added thoughtfully 'I suppose change is sometimes necessary for practical reasons. Princess did explain that because of the twins they'd had to buy a much bigger car, which is why the hedge had to go. It barely left enough room to open the doors of their new people carrier.'

'It makes sense. They seem a nice friendly couple. I think we'll get on alright don't you?'

'A bit different from Reg, but yes I think we will,' his wife agreed, adding wistfully, 'I wonder if they'll be looking for anyone to babysit those lovely twins?'

Night Falls

Sally Rich

The last rays of the sun pushed through the grimy windowpane, dust motes twisting and twirling in a complex dance as the light made its way to the floor. The shed was quiet, peaceful. A little fawn coloured mouse thrust her nose out from behind the bristle broom leaning in the corner, her black whiskers twitching to search out danger. Reassured she ventured to investigate the biscuit crumbs on the floor. They tasted good and she settled to munch her way through, pausing every now and then to wash her face and whiskers with the soft, suede-like pads of her front paws.

A fat brown spider made its lazy way down a thread from the wooden ceiling, legs flailing, determined to reach the top of the old table, a good anchor for the web. The table, chips and gouges across its surface, dust and old mud speckling the honey brown of the balsa, was home to boxes jumbled with trowels and forks poking this way and that. Old seed packets scattered among the boxes, their torn and jagged edges testament to the old man's habit of ripping them open in frustration at his inability to find his knife in all the mess. A small spirit stove held a kettle, still warm from the boiling. Under the table, terracotta and plastic pots of all shapes and sizes lay jumbled at crazy angles; dried-out threads of root and clumps of earth clinging to their insides. It had been some time since he had found the energy, even the will, to return his shed to the clean and tidy working space he had always been so proud of. It had matched his garden with its straight rows of vegetables, neat flower beds and the lawn always mown in regimented stripes. That had all gone by the board too. Weeds had even forced their way up through the paving cracks now.

In those earlier times he had been a stalwart of the local Garden Club; his vegetables and flowers winning prizes. Younger members would seek his advice at the monthly meetings. Why had their onions bolted? What rose should they buy that would fill their patio with fragrance throughout the summer? Endless questions. Sometimes he couldn't answer, but most times he would mutter a soft 'Aah' and dredge something up from his vast knowledge and they would walk away happy. He hadn't been able to get along to the meetings this last year, he was always too weary to venture out in the evenings. The chairwoman had been around a couple of times early on, but it was several months now since anyone had knocked on his front door. His shed had become his hideaway, comforting, familiar, safe.

A gust of wind rattled the door in its frame, whisking a few dried-up yellow leaves across the wooden boards. A brief spatter of raindrops on the sunlit window turned the dusty floor into a brilliant rainbow. The mouse scampered back to its hiding place behind the broom. The spider continued its weaving, unperturbed, backwards and forwards along the threads, an unseen trap for unwary flies.

The old man didn't move. His red and white striped woolly hat clung to his head, valiantly attempting its task of keeping him warm despite his baldness. His dark green fleece, unzipped, his greasy, grey t-shirt strained across the paunch of his belly. Baggy brown cords, held together by dirt and tucked into black wellies caked with old mud, revealed a crease of papery knee through the frayed material. His worn and lined face, wrinkled around the eyes and cheeks, crumpled into the folds of his chin. One hand rested on the green velveteen arm of the old stuffed chair, the other held a cup half full of mahogany tea, growing cold now.

The mouse ventured out of her hiding place again to resume her enjoyment of the biscuit crumbs. The man's eyes were open, staring at the mouse, but he could no longer see her. The cup slipped out of his hand, the tea cascading over his trouser legs, but he did not move. The mouse scampered back to the safety of the broom. The last rays of the sun disappeared from the window. The spider continued its weaving, unperturbed. Peace and silence settled over the shed again.